Babies on the Move

Susan Canizares
Daniel Moreton

Scholastic Inc.
New York • Toronto • London • Auckland • Sydney

Acknowledgments

Literacy Specialist: Linda Cornwell

Social Studies Consultant: Barbara Schubert, Ph.D.

Design: Silver Editions

Photo Research: Silver Editions

Endnotes: Jacqueline Smith

Endnote Illustrations: Anthony Carnabucia

Photographs: Cover: Bertrand Rieger/Tony Stone Images; p. 1: Stephen R. Swinburne/Stock Boston; p. 2: Yann Layma/Tony Stone Images; p. 3: Bertrand Rieger/Tony Stone Images; p. 4: George Holton/Photo Researchers, Inc.; p. 5: M. Greenlar/The Image Works: p. 6: Connie Coleman/Tony Stone Images; p. 7: Marie Breton/Rapho/Photo Researchers, Inc.; p. 8: David R. Austen/Stock Boston; p. 9: John Fortunato/Tony Stone Images; p. 10: Cary Wolinski/Tony Stone Images; p. 11: David Levy/Tony Stone Images; p. 12: Robert E. Daemmrich/Tony Stone Images.

Library of Congress Cataloging-in-Publication Data
Canizares, Susan, 1960-
Babies on the move / Susan Canizares, Daniel Moreton.
p. cm. -- (Social studies emergent readers)
Summary: Simple phrases and photographs show the ways that babies travel in different parts of the world, including baskets, blankets, sleds, and car seats.
ISBN 0-439-04556-8 (pbk.: alk. paper)
1. Infant carriers--Juvenile literature. [1. Infant carriers.]
I. Moreton, Daniel. II Title. III. Series.
GT24657.C36 1998
392.1'3--dc21   98-54251
                                                                              CIP AC

4   5   6   7   8   9   10   08   03   02

Babies on the move.

Babies in baskets.

Babies in blankets

and papooses.

Babies in strollers.

Babies on sleds

and in car seats.

Babies on backs.

And babies on their feet!

Babies on the Move

All over the world, babies must be carried or transported. Mothers and fathers have to go places, and they need a safe way to bring their babies with them. In many parts of the world, mothers, fathers, or siblings carry babies on their backs, fronts, or hips. This leaves their hands free to work and carry things, and babies feel comforted being next to a warm body. In other parts of the world, different kinds of "baby vehicles" are used.

Sled In Northern Europe and other cold and snowy places, pulling children on a sled was a very good way to move across the snow. Nowadays people don't just use sleds to transport children in their everyday lives—they do it just for fun!

Car seat Car seats are modern inventions. They are special seats for babies and children that get buckled into the car. Small babies can't sit up, so they travel lying down in car seats, which look a little bit like baskets or cradles. Car seats for bigger kids are usually high so the children can see out the window and the adults in the front can see what the children are doing! In the U.S., most states have laws requiring children up to four years old to travel in a car seat.

Stroller Strollers are also modern inventions, but they are based on baby carriages, which are over 100 years old. In baby carriages, babies lie down, but in strollers babies can sit up and see the world around them. Strollers are popular in places like the United States and Europe. In some Asian countries, strollers are made of bamboo, a common plant there.

Basket In the rainforest, baskets are one good way to keep children safe and up off the ground, where they might hurt themselves or run into dangerous animals, insects, or plants. In the forests of China, the Dong people keep children suspended safely in baskets while they farm. The Dayak women of Indonesia make beautiful baby baskets that they wear on their backs, leaving their hands free to work.

Blanket Another way to carry babies is in a blanket, tied onto the back or the hip. When the baby is not being carried, the blanket can be used to keep the baby warm.

Papoose Cradleboards (sometimes called papooses) were once used by most Native American tribes in North America. Today, papooses are used mainly for ceremonial purposes. The back is made of wood, tree branches, or reeds. The baby fits in the attached pouch, which is made from animal skin or cloth. The cradleboard was the baby's bed at night, and was strapped onto the mother's back during the day.

Back Babies are carried on people's backs all over the world in different kinds of carriers. Peruvian women keep their babies warm in colorful wool shawls. The baby backpack found in many places like the United States has a metal frame, plastic buckles, and nylon material.

Feet Carrying or transporting babies becomes less important when they start to walk, from about 9 months to 15 months. Walking is something we consider easy and natural, but babies have to work very hard to learn how to do it. First they begin to stand, holding on to things. Then they begin letting go, and stand for a few seconds before falling to the ground. Gradually, they get steadier on their feet. Finally, they take their first steps into the world, and for their parents it's as exciting as for the child herself!